Anthony Browne

WILLY THE CHAMP

Dragonfly Books • Alfred A. Knopf
New York

A DRAGONFLY BOOK PUBLISHED BY ALFRED A. KNOPF, INC.

Copyright © 1985 by Anthony Browne
All rights reserved under International and Pan-American
Copyright Conventions. Published in the United States
by Alfred A. Knopf, Inc., New York, and simultaneously
in Canada by Random House of Canada Limited, Toronto.
Distributed by Random House, Inc., New York.
Originally published in Great Britain by Julia MacRae Books,
a division of Franklin Watts, London, in 1985.
First American edition published in hardcover as a Borzoi Book by
Alfred A. Knopf, Inc., in 1986.

Library of Congress Card Number: 94-78855
ISBN: 0-679-87391-0
First Dragonfly Books edition: March 1995

Manufactured in Hong Kong
10 9 8 7 6 5 4 3 2 1

For Ellen

Willy didn't seem to be any good at anything.

He liked to read . . .

and listen to music . . .

and walk in the park with his friend, Millie.

Willy wasn't any good at soccer . . .

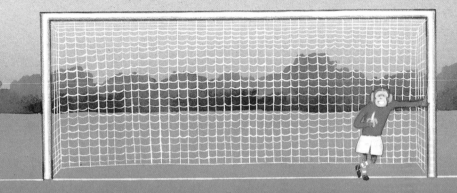

He did try.

Willy tried bike racing . . .

He really did try.

Sometimes Willy walked to the pool.

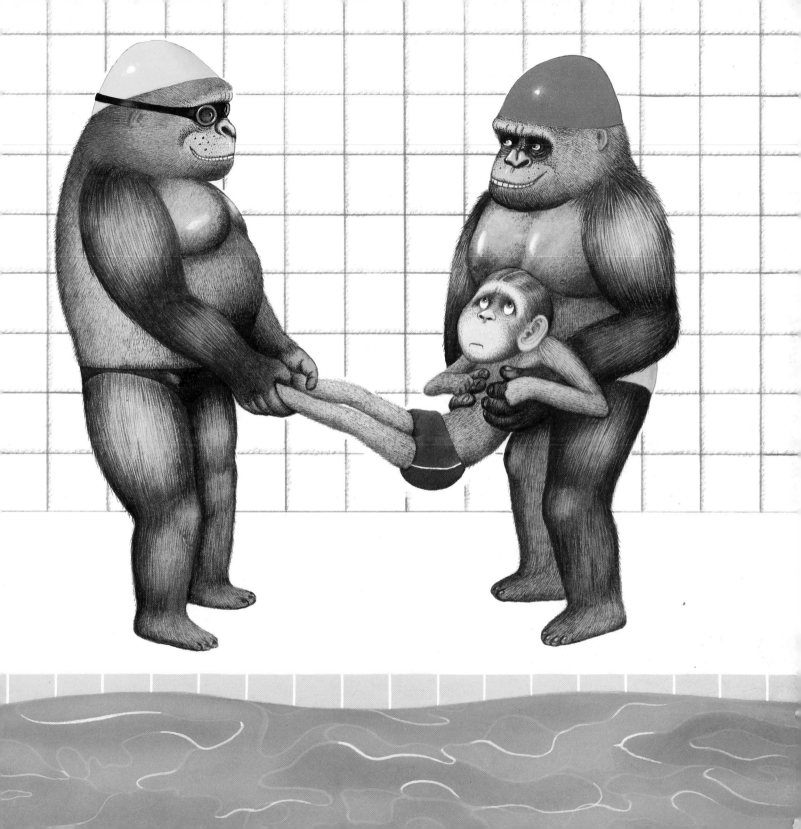

Other times he went to the movies with Millie.

But it was always the same. Nearly everyone
laughed at him – no matter what he did.

One day Willy was standing on the corner with the boys when a horrible figure appeared.

It was Buster Nose.
And he *had* a horrible figure.
The boys fled.

Buster threw a vicious punch.

Willy ducked . . .

then he stood up!

"Oh, I'm sorry," said Willy, "are you all right?"

Buster went home to his mom.

Willy was the Champ.